Precious Princess

The Bridesmaid Village Fair

Rebecca Parkinson

CWR

The Bridesmaid

Grandad always said that Daisy was his pretty, precious princess. That's why he gave her a special present.

'Daisy,' he said, 'precious princesses should learn precious secrets. This book will teach you many of the things you need to know as you grow up in this world. Read it well.'

It was then that the adventures began …

Daisy hopped from one foot to the other in excitement. She had been looking forward to this day for such a long time and at last it had arrived! She skipped to the window and peered out just as a car pulled into the driveway.

'Mum,' she shouted, running to open the front door. 'They're here!'

Auntie Rachel jumped out of the car and ran to give Daisy a hug.

'How's my favourite little bridesmaid?' she asked, lifting Daisy in the air and swinging her round.

'I'm your *only* little bridesmaid,' Daisy laughed, climbing into the back seat behind Grandma.

Mum climbed in beside her and soon they were off, leaving Dad and Jack waving on the doorstep.

Daisy sighed happily. At last she was going to get her dress. She couldn't think of anything better. She had spent hours imagining what it would be like. She didn't really mind what colour it was, although she liked the idea of lilac. But she really hoped it would have lots of layers of netting under the skirt so it would stick out at the sides, just like her best friend Katie had when she was a bridesmaid.

Daisy was too busy dreaming about her dress to hear what the grown-ups were talking about. This was going to be the best day ever!

To Daisy's surprise Auntie Rachel pulled up outside a cafe and stopped the engine.

'What are we doing?' Daisy asked, craning her neck to see if there was a dress shop round the back.

'I didn't think you were listening in the car,' laughed Mum. 'Auntie Rachel wants to stop here for a while to go through the wedding plans with us. There's such a lot to sort out and she wants a bit of help.'

'Oh,' said Daisy trying not to look as disappointed as she felt. 'How long will we be?'

'I'm not sure,' said Mum frowning. 'But remember this is Auntie Rachel and Uncle Mark's special day, so don't start moaning.'

For a short while Daisy was happy sitting at an outside table eating biscuits and drinking lemonade. But she soon started to fidget. This wasn't at all how she had imagined the day. She couldn't understand how anyone could be so interested in flowers, photographs, food, hotels and even cars.

'Can we go soon?' she whispered to Mum for the fifth time.

Mum frowned at her.

'Look Daisy,' she said in the quiet voice that meant Daisy was in trouble. 'This is Auntie Rachel's special day – it isn't all about you.'

Mum handed Daisy a bag.

'I thought this might happen,' she whispered. 'So I've put some things in here for you to do. Why don't you go and sit by that tree and have a look.'

Daisy leant against the tree trunk and opened the bag. To her surprise, among the colouring books and pens, Mum had put Grandad's special book.

Daisy lifted it out and flicked through the pages. The title of one of the stories caught her eye and she began to read …

Suddenly the tree began to spin. Daisy felt tingles running through her body. She could hear gentle music. She shut her eyes tight. This had happened before … where would she end up this time?

When Daisy opened her eyes she found that she was wearing a long dress made of silky material and she had new sandals on her feet. She was standing in a narrow street which was beautifully decorated with bright lamps. Daisy could hear loud music coming from a house so she crept forward hoping to see what was happening. She had just stretched up to peep through the window when the door opened and a man stepped into the street. As quick as a flash, Daisy slipped inside.

At the far end of the room Daisy could see two people seated under an archway covered with a mass of flowers. She knew at once that they were the bride and groom and that she had just walked into a party to celebrate their wedding!

The house was full of people laughing and dancing together. Daisy joined in until she spotted a group of worried looking servants, huddled in a corner. She tiptoed nearer.

'What are we going to do?' whispered one servant. 'I can't believe we've run out of drinks at a wedding. We mustn't tell the bride and groom. It's so embarrassing!'

   'Well it's too late to go and buy any more,' added another. 'But it's going to spoil the wedding if we just give everybody water.'

It was then that Daisy noticed an older lady standing close by. It was obvious that she too had been listening to the servants' conversation. As Daisy watched, the woman walked across the room towards a group of men and gently touched one of them on the arm.

'Jesus,' she said quietly. 'They've run out of wine.'

Jesus moved a short distance away from the group.

'What do you want me to do about it, Mother?' Jesus asked kindly. 'People don't yet know who I am or what I can do.'

Daisy saw Jesus look across the room to where the bride and groom were seated and then at the other wedding guests. She could see from the look of concern on His face that He understood the problem.

Jesus' mother beckoned one of the servants.

'Do whatever He tells you to do,' she said, nodding towards Jesus.

Jesus glanced round and pointed to six large pots standing in the shade.

'Go and fill those up with water,' He said.

The servants looked confused, but they hurried to do what Jesus said and soon returned carrying the heavy pots.

'Now go and give a cupful to the man in charge of the wedding,' said Jesus.

The servants looked at each other in surprise but after thinking about it for a moment they poured a cup of water from the pots.

Slowly, with a terrified look on his face, one of the servants carried the cup across the room to an important looking man. The man took the cup in his hands and drank a big mouthful.

The servants held their breath, waiting for trouble!

As Daisy watched, a look of complete amazement spread across the man's face.

'Wow!' he exclaimed, beckoning the groom over to him. 'This is delicious! Usually people serve the best wine at the start of a party. But you've saved the best until now.'

Daisy stood for a moment watching the different people. The groom looked confused but happy. The servants were shaking their heads as if unable to believe what they had just seen. Jesus' friends were whispering to each other, obviously shocked that one of their friends had done something so amazing. But Jesus wasn't making a big fuss. Instead, He just looked quietly happy that He had been able to help make a wedding day special for people He cared about.

Suddenly Daisy felt tingles running through her body. The loud wedding music changed to gentle music and things began to spin. She shut her eyes tight …

When Daisy opened her eyes she was back, leaning against the tree with Grandad's book resting on her knee.

She looked across to where the grown-ups were still busy talking. She felt a little bit selfish when she remembered the look on Jesus' face. He hadn't wanted to be the centre of attention. He had simply cared about two friends getting married and had been willing to do anything to help make their wedding wonderful. Suddenly Daisy understood.

This was Auntie Rachel and Uncle Mark's special day and they wanted *everything* to be as perfect as possible. The most important thing wasn't her dress. It was about everyone helping to make this the best wedding day ever!

Daisy jumped up and skipped across to the table.

'What can I do to help?' she asked, climbing on to Auntie Rachel's knee. 'I don't mind doing anything.'

Auntie Rachel and Grandma smiled at her and Mum look relieved.

'Just keep that lovely smile on your face,' said Auntie Rachel, tickling Daisy in the ribs. 'And then, even if everything else goes wrong, I'll still have the most beautiful bridesmaid in the world!'

Daisy looked at Auntie Rachel's face. Suddenly she felt all tingly inside. This time it wasn't the start of a new adventure, but the knowledge that she was helping to make someone else very happy.

Why not read this story in your own Bible? You will find it in Bible book John, chapter 2 verses 1 to 12.

Village Fair

Grandad always said that Daisy was his pretty, precious princess. That's why he gave her a special present.

'Daisy,' he said, 'precious princesses should learn precious secrets. This book will teach you many of the things you need to know as you grow up in this world. Read it well.'

It was then that the adventures began …

'*Mum!*' screeched Daisy, leaving the front door wide open as she ran into the house. '*Mum!*'

Mum raced out of the kitchen looking flustered.

'What is it Daisy?' she asked. 'What's happened?'

'I've just seen someone putting a poster up,' Daisy panted. 'And you'll never guess who's coming to open the village fair this year.'

Mum made a few suggestions but Daisy shook her head.

'No, you're wrong.' said Daisy, her eyes shining. 'It's Alex, the man who's on nearly every programme on television.'

'Wow!' said Mum, sounding impressed. 'The organisers have done well to get him. It should bring crowds of people, he's really famous.'

At last the day of the village fair arrived. Daisy was up early.

'Pleeeeeeease hurry up!' she begged, watching Mum frantically trying to fasten Jack into his pushchair.

'We're nearly ready,' laughed Mum, clicking the catch into place. 'But Daisy, don't get too excited. There'll be so many people at the fair that you'll probably not even see Alex.'

'But I might.' said Daisy, hoping that Mum would be wrong.

When Daisy arrived at the fair she stared in dismay at the crowds of people. It felt like everyone in the world had come to see Alex.

Suddenly a voice spoke through the loudspeaker.

'If you'd like to make your way to the main stage, the fair will be officially opened in five minutes.'

'Come on,' said Mum, grabbing Daisy's hand and starting to run.

By the time they reached the stage area, hundreds of people had gathered and Alex was nothing but a tiny figure in the distance. Daisy couldn't even see if it was really him. She wanted to cry.

'Never mind,' said Mum. 'Come on, let's go and enjoy the fair anyway.'

Daisy soon forgot about her disappointment in the noise and excitement of the fair. Everywhere she looked there was something new to see or do: bouncy castles and giant slides, swing boats, a coconut shy, stalls selling everything from candy floss to beautiful crafts. Daisy loved everything, but her favourite was the Victorian merry-go-round, which played old-fashioned music as the beautifully painted horses rode up and down.

'I think we should go soon,' said Mum, as she finished eating an ice-cream. 'Jack's getting tired and I think we've seen everything.'

'Aww,' groaned Daisy. 'Please can I just go on one more thing?'

Mum nodded.

'One more,' she said. 'And then no moaning!'

'OK,' said Daisy. 'I'll go on 'hook-a-duck'. I didn't go on that before 'cos the queue was too long.'

Daisy held the wooden pole in two hands and concentrated as hard as she could on hooking one of the plastic ducks bobbing on the water.

'Yes!' she shouted after a few seconds, lifting the duck in the air. 'Got it!'

'Well done.' said a man's voice behind her. 'You're good at that.'

Daisy turned to see who was speaking. Her mouth fell wide open. There, about two steps away, stood Alex!

Alex smiled when he saw Daisy's face.

'I seem to have that effect on a lot of people,' he laughed. 'My name is Alex and I'm pleased to meet you.'

Alex held out his hand and Daisy shook it shyly.

'Daisy was hoping she'd meet you,' said Mum. 'She's quite a fan of yours. Would you mind if I took a photograph of you and her together?'

Alex stood next to Daisy as Mum took a picture with her phone.

'Can we print it out as soon as we get home?' Daisy asked, finding her voice again as soon as Alex had walked away.

Mum nodded.

'Of course we can,' she said. 'What a lovely surprise.'

At bedtime, Daisy placed the photograph of herself and Alex on her bedside table. She couldn't wait to show her friends. She couldn't believe that she had met someone so famous!

Daisy sat down on her bed. It had been such a busy day and she felt tired. She picked up Grandad's special book and began to turn the pages. The title of one of the stories caught her eye and slowly she began to read …

Suddenly the room began to spin. Daisy felt tingles running through her body. She could hear gentle music. She shut her eyes tight. This had happened before … where would she end up this time?

When Daisy opened her eyes she was wearing a dress that reached down to her ankles and she had sandals on her feet. She was standing beside a road at the front of a large crowd of people. Everyone was peering in the same direction and talking in excited voices.

'Jesus is on His way.'

'He'll be here soon!'

It was then that Daisy noticed a woman standing at her side. The woman's head was covered with a scarf that she had pulled round her pale face as if she didn't want to be noticed. Her back was hunched and Daisy could see that she was very sick. The woman was glancing round nervously as if trying to decide what to do.

'I can see Him!' yelled someone in the crowd.

Jesus and His friends walked right in front of the place where Daisy was standing. As they passed, Daisy saw the woman gaze up at Jesus, a glimmer of hope appearing on her face. The woman stepped forward to join the crowd following Jesus along the road. Daisy followed too, wondering what the woman was about to do.

As the crowd pushed and shoved, hoping to get closer to Jesus, Daisy saw the woman glance from side to side. Then slowly she raised her arm, stretched out her hand and gently touched the bottom of Jesus' cloak.

Immediately, Daisy saw the woman stand up straight. A smile lit up her face, she looked well and healthy. Daisy was amazed!

The woman turned and began to push her way through the crowd, but suddenly Jesus stopped and spoke in a loud voice.

'Who touched me?' He asked, looking round.

Jesus' friends laughed at Him.

'There are so many people here!' they said. 'Anyone could have touched you.'

The crowd nodded in agreement, but Daisy knew that Jesus was right. She saw the woman stop and turn to look at Him. For a moment Daisy thought the woman wasn't going to own up, but suddenly she ran forward and knelt on the floor in front of Jesus.

'It was me who touched you,' she said quietly. 'I've been ill for twelve years. I've seen loads of doctors and spent all my money trying to get better, but nothing has worked. I'd heard about you and I thought that you were so powerful that if I just touched your cloak I'd get better. So that's what I did. I touched your cloak and I knew straight away that I was better. Thank you!'

Jesus smiled down at the woman.

'You'll have no more pain and suffering now,' He said. 'Get up and go in peace.'

The woman stood up. Daisy could see that all the fear and sickness had completely disappeared. She looked like a totally different person!

Suddenly Daisy felt tingles running through her body. She could hear gentle music again and things began to spin. She shut her eyes tight …

When Daisy opened her eyes she was sitting back on her bed with Grandad's book resting on her knee. For a moment she thought about what she had just seen. The woman must have left home that day hoping that she would meet Jesus, in the same way that Daisy had hoped to see Alex at the village fair. Daisy looked at the photograph of the two of them standing together with the 'hook-a-duck' in the background. She was sure she'd keep the picture forever!

Daisy lay back on her bed and gazed up at the ceiling. It had been so exciting to meet someone famous but it couldn't even begin to compare with meeting Jesus. After all, meeting Jesus changed people's lives forever!

Daisy smiled as she closed her eyes, it had been a wonderful day.

Why not read this story in your own Bible? You will find it in Bible book Mark, chapter 5 verses 25 to 34.

The Bridesmaid + Village Fair

For Reanne.
With love x

OTHER TITLES IN THIS SERIES INCLUDE:

Precious Princess: Ballerina Necklace/The Birthday Present
Precious Princess: Starry Night/On the Beach
Precious Princess: New Girl/The Picnic

Copyright text © Rebecca Parkinson 2013
Copyright illlustrations © CWR 2013

Published 2013 by CWR, Waverley Abbey House, Waverley Lane, Farnham, Surrey GU9 8EP, UK. CWR is a Registered Charity – Number 294387 and a Limited Company registered in England – Registration Number 1990308.

The right of Rebecca Parkinson to be identified as the author of this work has been asserted by her in accordance with the Copyright, Designs and Patents Act 1988 sections 77 and 78.

Visit www.cwr.org.uk/distributors for a list of National Distributors
Concept development, editing, design and production by CWR
Illustrations by Mike Henson at CWR
Printed and bound in China by C&C Offset Printing Co.,Ltd
ISBN: 978-1-78259-149-8